SI

AND
SLIPPERY
SAM

The Aliens Are Coming!

TRACEY CORDEROY
STEVEN LENTON

nosy crow

First published in the UK in 2019 by Nosy Crow Ltd
The Crow's Nest, 14 Baden Place, Crosby Row,
London, SE1 1YW, UK

Nosy Crow and associated logos are trademarks and/or registered
trademarks of Nosy Crow Ltd

1 3 5 7 9 10 8 6 4 2

A CIP catalogue record for this book will be available from the British Library.

Printed in Spain

Papers used by Nosy Crow are made from wood grown in
sustainable forests.

ISBN: 978 1 78800 152 6

www.nosycrow.com

CONTENTS

For Mark, thank you for
your belief and support.
T.C. x

For Ola Gotkowska.
S.L. x

Shifty McGifty and Slippery Sam

don't just make AMAZING cakes. These two brave bakers solve wacky mysteries too! Trouble might be just around the corner but Shifty and Sam are always ready...

The Aliens Are Coming!

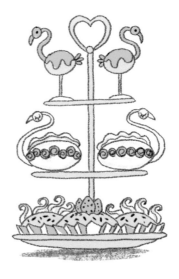

Chapter One

One sunny afternoon Shifty and Sam were in the park, thinking up new recipes. Shifty was thinking quietly on the grass. And Sam was thinking as he whizzed down the slide!

But then Sam went a bit too fast, flew off the end and – crash!

Sam rubbed his bumped head. For a moment he saw stars. Then Sam saw little aliens. Two bright-green ones, running in and out of the trees.

Sam tiptoed to Shifty.

"Psst," whispered Sam. "Shifty! Alien attack!"

"Eh? Funny name for a cake!" snorted Shifty, his head still buried in his notebook.

"N-no, alien attack's not a recipe," spluttered Sam. "There are aliens – over in the trees!"

Shifty looked over. There was nothing there. Then he saw a big lump on Sam's head.

"Hey, Sam – are you OK?!" Shifty gasped. "You bumped your head and now you're seeing things."

"I'm not!" Sam frowned. "I really did see aliens."

Shifty closed his notebook. "So where's their flying saucer?"

"I dunno." Sam shrugged. "Probably hidden! We need to get out of here – fast!"

Tutting, Shifty gathered up their things. "Come on then, let's go home," he said, hoping Sam would forget all about the "aliens".

As they walked back through town Sam was quiet. Why wouldn't Shifty believe him?

"I need to get a book," said Sam as they passed the library, "on what to do when aliens ATTACK!"

"I'll wait here," sighed Shifty as Sam pattered inside.

The library was busy. Sam found the "Outer Space" section but all the shelves were BARE!

"Grrr," grumbled Sam. "Who's nabbed all the space books?!"

Then he saw them again. The aliens from the park! But there were more of them now, and bigger ones too. And their arms were piled high with space books.

"Whoa!" gasped Sam. "Wait till I tell Shifty. He'll have to believe me now!"

Chapter Two

"MORE aliens!" shouted Sam, darting back out. "And they're hogging ALL the space books too! Now no one will have a clue what to do when they ATTACK!"

Sam tried dragging Shifty to see. But Shifty was having none of it.

"You need to get home to rest," said Shifty, helping Sam off down the street.

"But! But!" spluttered Sam.

"No buts," said Shifty. "I'm worried about you."

But back at home Sam would NOT rest. He decided that the garden shed would make a brilliant safety bunker for when the aliens attacked. First, though, he had to alien-proof it.

It took ages, but by bedtime Sam had done it. He rushed Shifty out to see.

"Ta-daaa!" cried Sam. Shifty's jaw dropped. Sam had foil-wrapped the ENTIRE garden!

"It'll stop alien spaceships landing," smiled Sam. "'Cos it'll dazzle them. Plus, it's non-stick."

"Poo!" Shifty frowned. "What's that smell?"

"Oh! That's my alien-repellent necklace," beamed Sam. "But don't worry, I made one for you too!" And he popped the stinky garlic necklace over Shifty's head. "It stops aliens coming too close," nodded Sam.

"And anyone else!" Shifty shuddered,
holding his nose.

Sam had stuck up lots of TV aerials too to confuse any flying-saucer trackers. And on the door of the "safety bunker", Sam had nailed a notice...

NIBBITY
NIIB
NOO!

"It's ALIEN SPEAK," he explained. "It means: 'Aliens keep OUT!'"

Shifty looked at him. "Have you made that up?"

"No!" frowned Sam. "Well – yes – but I had to! Because the aliens took all the space books, remember?"

That night the boys got NO sleep at all. At every creak, Sam boomed, "Alien attack!" and rugby-tackled Shifty to the floor.

"What are you doing?!" hissed Shifty.

"Taking cover," tutted Sam. "Obviously!"

By morning Shifty was exhausted. And he stank of garlic too. "Right, seeing as they DIDN'T attack," he grumbled, "I'm off for a bath, then I'm opening the café."

"Are you crazy?!" called Sam.

"If anyone's crazy round here," muttered Shifty, "it's not ME!"

Sam stayed down the shed until just before café closing time when his "emergency provisions" (jam doughnuts) ran out. Then he risked it inside to snaffle more.

There was only one customer left in the café when Sam sneaked in. Matilda was just finishing off her coffee, when—

"SHIFTY!" shrieked Sam.
He pointed a paw.
"THERE!!"

Heading through the door were two tall aliens. Sam whisked out his cupcake catapult at once and Shifty swiftly tossed him a cupcake. But Matilda, Sam noticed, hadn't batted an eyelid.

21

"Matilda! Aliens!" shouted Sam. Then one of the aliens spoke…

"Hello! I don't suppose you happen to have a cake in the shape of a flying saucer, do you?"

"A big one! To feed HUNDREDS," the other alien nodded.

"Maybe with popping-candy sprinkles?"

Chapter
Three

Sam winked at Shifty so he'd play along.

These aliens were a right cunning bunch!
They'd even learned polite EARTH SPEAK to
trick everyone into believing they were nice!

Sam said that they would bake them an alien
cake and that it would be ready in an hour.
The aliens beamed and, antennae bobbing
brightly, they left.

"Um, r-right," stuttered Shifty. "We need to

tail them
– quick."

"Sure!" squeaked Sam. "But that
alien said there were HUNDREDS of them!"

Grabbing some of Sam's "alien-capturing"
gadgets, they left Matilda to lock up the café.

"No – wait!" Matilda shouted after them. "I
need to go to the schoo—"

But Shifty and Sam were already through the
door. Wherever Matilda needed to go was no
way as important as this!

They followed the aliens down the road

and into the
local primary school.
Keeping a safe distance, they crept in
behind them and hid behind some coats in the
cloakroom. Their laser-beam baguettes were at
the ready in case things turned nasty.

Every single classroom along the corridor
was jam-packed with excitable little aliens.

"Eeeek!" gulped Sam. "Looks like they can't wait to attack."

The boys saw the two tall aliens from the café hurry into the school hall. Then suddenly the staffroom door burst open and more tall aliens rushed out into the classrooms, making loud hissing noises until all the little aliens fell silent.

"See?" whispered Sam. "ALIEN SPEAK. I told you!"

All the little aliens lined up by the door and were marched into the school hall too. When the coast was clear, Shifty and Sam sneaked outside to the back door of the hall and quietly slipped inside.

"I bet," whispered Sam, "they beamed the hall roof open and they're hiding their flying saucer in here!"

"Well, Sam," whispered Shifty, "we'll soon see."

They crept on through a tangle of long black curtains. Up ahead they could see a beam of green light. Then they heard some weird, creepy music.

"Ready to get those aliens then?" whispered Shifty. But Sam had a mouthful of laser-beam baguette.

"Ooo – sorry!" Sam swallowed. "Aliens … always make me hungry."

"Right," nodded Shifty.

"Charrrggge!"

Chapter Four

The boys charged forward swishing their lasers.

And then they saw it –

– the aliens' flying saucer, and tons of little aliens all round it!!

"Y-you'd better come q-quietly, you … aliens," warned Shifty. "'Cos Sam's a dab hand with a laser!"

"I am??" Sam gulped. "Oh yeah – I AM!"

But before Sam could show them what he was made of...

"Sam's funny!" a little alien giggled. The boys knew that voice. It was Henrietta. One of Matilda's puppies!

Then Shifty saw that they were on ... a stage. He peered into the middle of the gloomy hall, where he could just make out chairs, and folk sitting on them.

"Psst! Sam!" said Shifty under his breath. But Sam had seen them too. And there in the front row sat Matilda.

"Shifty, do you think what I think?" whispered Sam.

"I think I do," Shifty whispered back. Those folk on the chairs were the audience, and the aliens on stage weren't aliens at all, but schoolpups and schoolteachers dressed up.

"So...?" Sam blushed.

"Yup," nodded Shifty. "We're in the ... school play." Then they both saw the banner on the PRETEND flying saucer...

ALIENS THE

"Uh-oh," gulped Sam. Now everything made sense. The two little aliens he'd spotted in the park must have gone there after rehearsing for the play, still in their alien costumes.

And the ones in the library must have needed all the space books as part of the big school project.

Finally, that was why Matilda hadn't been scared of the tall aliens in the café earlier. She'd known all along that they were just teachers – dressed up!

"What on earth are you doing?" came a voice, and a teacher in an alien onesie stomped

MUSICAL!

up, his ping-pong-
ball antennae bobbing
wildly.

"W-we just…" began
Shifty. But suddenly he
got stage fright.

"RUN!"

35

The boys belted it back to the café. But then they felt so bad. They'd completely wrecked the opening of the school play.

"Wait!" cried Sam. "To show that we're sorry, how about we make them that cake?"

"Brilliant!" smiled Shifty.

So that's what they did! And by the time the play was over, an out-of-this-world flying-saucer cake was waiting for everyone backstage.

One little "pup", in the most AMAZING costume, tucked in like he'd never seen cake before! In four nanoseconds flat he was on his third slice…

"Nibbity! Nibbity! Burp!!"

Ice-Cream Time

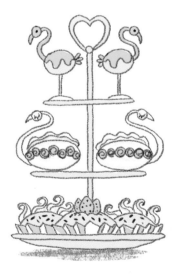

Chapter One

The sun was shining, kites were flying, and Shifty and Sam were at the seaside.

"Come on, Sam," Shifty called. "It's time for the sandcastle competition!"

Sam came splashing from the sea. "Hooray!"

They joined a big crowd gathered on the sand, waiting for the competition to start. Some of their café customers were entering too.

First prize was a smart gold trophy in the shape of a bucket and spade. And competitors could build anything they liked, as long as it was made out of sand.

Next to Shifty and Sam was a little rabbit. "I'm making a giant sand carrot," he smiled. "What about you?"

"Oh, me and Sam are doing a cupcake!" replied Shifty.

"A cupcake??" came a voice, and up marched a red panda.

43

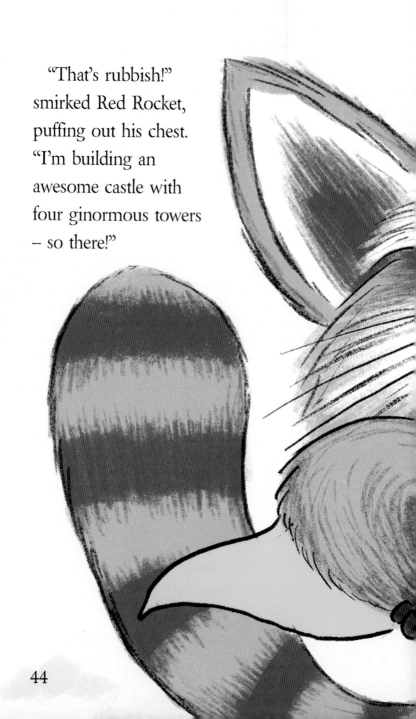

"That's rubbish!" smirked Red Rocket, puffing out his chest. "I'm building an awesome castle with four ginormous towers – so there!"

With that, the competition judge bumbled up.

"So sorry I'm late," puffed the old mole. "Lost my spectacles and still can't find them! Right, are you all ready – or even, um … there?" He peered around with tiny, squinty eyes.

"Yes!" cried everyone.

"Ah, good!" smiled the mole. "Then – ready – steady – DIG!"

47

Sand began flying everywhere as they all got stuck in. Shifty and Sam started making their cupcake, while Duchess began planning out a mermaid. Fred was doing a big vintage car, Scottie was making an octopus and Hercules was attempting an enormous Eiffel Tower!

Tutting, Red Rocket headed over a nearby sand dune to build his "awesome" sandcastle in private!

"Hmm…" muttered Shifty.

"Fishy," whispered Sam. "Why can't he build it out here where everyone can see him?"

But there wasn't time to worry about that now. There was too much to do. So Shifty and Sam, like everyone else, shovelled sand like crazy!

A whole hour later, when they stopped for a tea break, Shifty sneaked a peek over the sand dune. Red Rocket had his feet up and was reading a comic, not a whiff of a sandcastle anywhere.

"Where's his spade even?" muttered Shifty. Just what was Red Rocket up to...?

Chapter
Two

Shifty and Sam's giant sand cupcake was
beginning to look very smart. But then Shifty
spied Red Rocket on the move.

"Right, Sam, you stay here and I'll follow
him," he said, dishing out a pair of walkie-
talkies cunningly disguised as ice creams.

"Ooo – I bagsy the one with sprinkles!"
cried Sam, swapping them.

Shifty hurried off along the crowded beach,

peering through his BUN-oculars. Red Rocket had completely disappeared, which was never a good sign.

Half an hour later, Sam's walkie-talkie

buzzed and he heard Shifty's voice.

"Lobster to Pufferfish: just spotted Red: OVER."

"Pufferfish??" Sam frowned. "You know my codename's Stingray!" Sam shook his head as he heard Shifty laughing. "So where is he, Lobster?"

"Rock-pooling down by the caves."

"Roger, Lobster!" replied Sam. "OVER AND OUT!"

But before Sam could leave, some friends appeared, all holding brightly coloured buckets.

"Hi, Sam," said Duchess. "We're just off to collect shells to decorate our sand sculptures."

"Want to come too?" asked Hercules.

"Sure!" nodded Sam, grabbing his bucket. "But can we go by the caves? Shifty's there and he needs my help." The others gave a nod.

"No problem," Fred replied.

They headed off, collecting shells as they did, and some sticks and shiny pebbles.

"Hi, Shifty!" said Sam, when they got to the caves. "So where's Red Rocket then?"

Shifty pointed over to the rock-pools but Red Rocket had disappeared.

"He's gone," groaned Shifty.

"Oh," said Sam. "But look!" And he showed Shifty the shells he'd found. "To decorate our cupcake," explained Sam.

"Great for sprinkles!" Shifty smiled. And they decided to forget about trying to follow Red Rocket and go back with their friends to finish their sand sculptures instead.

On the way they passed Red Rocket's base. Red Rocket still wasn't there.

"And look!" cried Sam. "He STILL hasn't started his sandcastle!"

But then they got an even bigger surprise...

"Crabs!" yelled Hercules. There were dozens of them, scuttling all over their beautiful work, leaving great holes and gaping craters.

"How—" began Sam.

"More like WHO!" shouted Shifty. "What do rock-pools have? CRABS! And who's just been rock-pooling?"

"Grrr!" fumed Sam.

"Red Rocket!"

Chapter Three

With that, Fred spotted Red Rocket at the ice-cream van, pushing to the front of the queue.

They all marched up, furious.

"Cheat!" frowned Hercules. "You wrecked our lovely work!"

"PROVE IT!" smirked Red Rocket as he pushed past, slurping his ice lolly. "You had no chance of winning anyway. I'm gonna win so … pthhhhhhhh!" And, nose in the air, the fluffy red panda stomped off.

"We can't let him win!" rumbled Hercules.

"Don't worry," replied Shifty, "we won't!" And he hurried them all to the Bakemobile at once.

"Right, each of you find a cake slice," said Shifty. "They'll smooth out any holes those crabs made."

"Perfect!" cried Scottie.

"And I'll take this piping bag too," smiled Sam. He'd just had a brilliant idea!

Back on the beach, the cake slices worked a treat at smoothing out all the crabs' claw marks. Then Sam filled his piping bag up with damp sand.

"How about this then?" He smiled as he added a neat sandy swirl on the top of their lovely cupcake.

"It's lemon icing!" said Sam.

Then Shifty popped on some shells. "With sprinkles!"

When everyone had finished their decorating, there was time for a quick dip in the sea. On their way back, Scottie sneaked a peep to see how Red Rocket's "awesome" castle was coming on.

"He's still not even started it!" Scottie reported back. "So he'll never win now. There's no time!"

And sure enough, up bumbled the judge, bumping right into Sam.

"Ooops, sorry!" said the mole. "Still haven't found my specs. Anyway…"

He blew a whistle.

"Gather round, please!" he called. "It's judging time!"

Chapter
Four

Everybody put down their spades. Then the short-sighted mole was helped along to the first sand sculpture.

"Wonderful!" he said, squinting hard. "It looks just like a pug in a snorkel!"

"No, that is a pug in a snorkel," said the pug in the snorkel's mother. "His sandcastle is that big thing next to him."

"Oh, of course!" smiled the old mole.

He moved around, trying not to trample anything, and seemed to like everything he (almost) saw.

Finally he stopped at Shifty and Sam's sculpture.

"Ah yes – a splendid, um…"

"Cupcake!" said Shifty, helping him out.

"With a swirl of lemon icing and cockleshell sprinkles!" chipped in Sam.

The mole gave a very impressed-looking nod. "Right, I'd better announce the winner!" he exclaimed.

"Oi!" came a voice. "You haven't seen mine yet!" And Red Rocket glared down from the top of the sand dune.

The old mole looked from side to side. "Who said that?"

Sam turned him in the direction of the sand dune and the mole went bumbling over it. The curious crowd began to follow behind.

"It can't be much good," whispered Duchess. "He hadn't even started it ten minutes ago."

But Duchess was wrong.

Everyone gasped when they saw Red Rocket's sandcastle.

"It's—" Sam stopped. He could hardly believe his eyes. "It's … awesome!"

It was perfectly smooth, even glistening. And there were four very tall straight towers. It even had windows, and flags made from sand at the top.

"Told you!" said Red Rocket with a smirk.

"Even I can see this!" smiled the old mole. "It's magnificent! In fact – yes – I declare it the WINNER!"

Red Rocket had never looked more smug than when he was handed the gold trophy.

"Trust him to win," muttered Shifty. "But how did he manage to do it?"

"Dunno," answered Sam. "But something isn't right."

When no one was looking, Sam hurried across to take a closer look. But – "Whooops!" – he tripped over Red Rocket's bucket, flew through the air and – boing!!

He'd bounced off the sandcastle!

"Hang on!" Shifty said. "You don't bounce off sand…"

Shifty prodded the castle.

"It's a blow-up one!"

"Huh!" frowned Sam. "So that's how he 'built' it so quickly!"

Red Rocket was made to give back his trophy and let everyone have a go on his bouncy castle.

Then the old mole appeared with prizes for everyone.

"Ice-cream time!" cheered Sam. "Oh, I do like to be beside the seaside!"

Miss Peachy-Pie's Pamper Café

Chapter One

Shifty and Sam were twiddling their thumbs.
They had nothing better to do. And that's
because all week their café had been EMPTY!

Then who should Sam see coming down
the street with a gang of her posh friends, but
Duchess.

"Customers!" cheered Sam.

"At last!" Shifty smiled. But Duchess and her
friends swept straight past.

"Can't stop!" called Duchess. "Off to have lunch and get my nails painted while I eat!" They hurried off.

"Eh?" said Shifty. "What café does nail-painting around here?"

As Sam gave a shrug, Fred drove past – his car as shiny as glass.

"Nice day, boys!" he called. "I've just had the BEST coffee. Miss Peachy-Pie even washed my car as I drank it!"

"Miss Peachy-Pie?" Shifty narrowed his eyes. "Sounds like a new café's just opened."

"No wonder we've been empty all week," groaned Sam. "We need to take a look at this Peachy-Pie place. Come on!"

The boys headed off but were soon overtaken by a gang of excited Border collies.

"She's such a little star, that Miss Peachy-Pie," said one.

"Best café for miles!" smiled another.

"I'm having a trim and blow-dry with my lunch!" beamed a third.

"A blow-dry with lunch?" Sam shook his head. "Ridiculous!"

They followed the crowd into the poshest part of town where all the little shops were so fancy. They had chic wooden shutters, ice-cream-coloured canopies and lollipop-shaped rosebushes in flowerpots.

Then, at last, the boys saw what the fuss was all about. With a gasp they looked up at the very sparkly sign...

Hanging in the window was a long, gold-framed list of everything this café had to offer. And a lot of it was absolutely free.

Menu

FREE   Hair braids with milkshakes

FREE   Cucumber face masks with juice

FREE   Gel nails with lunch

FREE   Blow dry with mocktails

"Hey, Sam, what even IS a mocktail?" asked Shifty.

But Sam had disappeared.

"Sam??"

Chapter Two

"SAM!" gasped Shifty. "What are you doing?!"

Sam was inside Miss Peachy-Pie's café, having the time of his life! And he wasn't the only one either.

The place was jam-packed with happy-looking customers eating gorgeous-looking food and drinking yummy-looking drinks! And at the same time, they were all being pampered to the nines.

Some were having their nails done, or their hair trimmed and styled. And the stylists were all chic-looking cats in swish uniforms.

"Oh, Shifty!" beamed Sam. "You should try one of these. It's a Mango Mule Mocktail. Yum yum!"

Shifty gaped. "Sam, are you crazy? This café
will put ours out of business!"

There were cupcakes with every flavour topping you could think of, and eclairs in the shape of dainty swans. There were macaroons too – brightly coloured flamingo ones, and a huge smoothie bar with a sign that said:

Help yourself to everything – and MORE!

Their old café
customers were
looking so relaxed!
Rover was having
long colourful
hair braids,

while Duchess was
getting her nails
done.

Lady Woofington was there too, being styled for a party.

Even little Hercules was chilling out with a cucumber face mask!

97

"Time to go, Sam," frowned Shifty, whisking Sam to the door. But Miss Peachy-Pie caught up with them before they could head off.

"Free umbrellas, boys!" she said with a smile. "Just in case it rains. We don't want Sam's blow-dry going frizzy, now, do we?"

"Oooh, thanks!" beamed Sam.

But Shifty gave a tut. "Come on, Sam!"

They edged away from the perfectly turned-out cat, with her big twinkly smile and neat apron. But the moment they were out of earshot, Shifty glanced back.

"She's just too good to be true," he muttered.

"What do you mean?" asked Sam.

"There's just something fishy about Peachy-Pie's," said Shifty. "And if folk keep choosing this café and not ours, well ... it's going to be bad news."

99

"You mean…" Sam gaped and his bouncy curls flopped. "Our café will close? FOR GOOD?"

Shifty nodded sadly.

"Oh NO!" Sam turned pale. "That's terrible!"

Sam said he would think. Think of a way to make their café the BEST once more. It just needed to be bright, bold and "different".

"Like no other café around," said Sam. "Hmmm…"

Chapter Three

"Shifty! Shifty! I've done it!" whooped Sam. He waved a sheet of paper in the air. "Our café makeover plan." He tossed Shifty a paintbrush and opened the paint.

"Whoa! Isn't that a bit bright?" Shifty squinted at the jazzy colour.

"Nah," grinned Sam. "It's going to be awesome – trust me!"

They got started. By midnight their café was

a mess. But by morning…

"You're right, Sam!" Shifty exclaimed. "It IS awesome!"

Glowing with pride, Sam unveiled their new sign.

"THE DEALS ON WHEELS DINER!" read Shifty.

"See now," explained Sam, "we're a café AND a swap-shop. Our customers can bring in things they don't want, and swap them for things that they do."

THE DEALS ON WHEELS DINER

"They do deals!" cried Shifty.

"Exactly!" nodded Sam.

"And the 'wheels' bit?" asked Shifty. He pointed to their sign.

Sam ducked behind the counter then whizzed out on ... roller skates!

"The wheeeeeels bit!" squealed Sam, flying into a table – CRASH!!

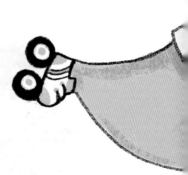

Pretty soon, all their old customers were back!

"Swap you my hanky for your twelve-gear mountain bike?" Scottie asked a whippet.

"Swap you these sprouts for your car, Fred?" asked Dotty. "They're full of vitamins – go on!"

Soon Peachy-Pie's Pamper Café was old news as Shifty and Sam's took top spot again.

"I LOVE it!" beamed Duchess, keen to swap her ruby ring for Lady Woofington's diamond tiara.

"Oh, but wait!" gasped Duchess. "Where is

my ruby ring?"

"And where's my tiara?!" shrieked Lady Woofington.

"And my tie pin?" frowned Rover.

"And my watch!" cried Hercules.

"And where's my spare car key?!" wondered Fred.

With that, Fred's car went zooming past the window. And the driver was a smart robber-cat!

"It's h-her!"
spluttered Shifty.
"Miss Peachy-Pie! I'd
recognise that twinkly
smile anywhere. All
that pampering stuff
was to make everyone
relaxed so that *her* lot
could steal all their
treasures."

"She's not any old
robber either," gulped
Sam. "She's a master of
disguise – look!"

He picked up Fred's
newspaper and waved
it in the air.

"The cat burglar –
Kitty Le Claw!"

THE

KITTY LE
CLAW!

She's kno
for disgui
and for b
the law.

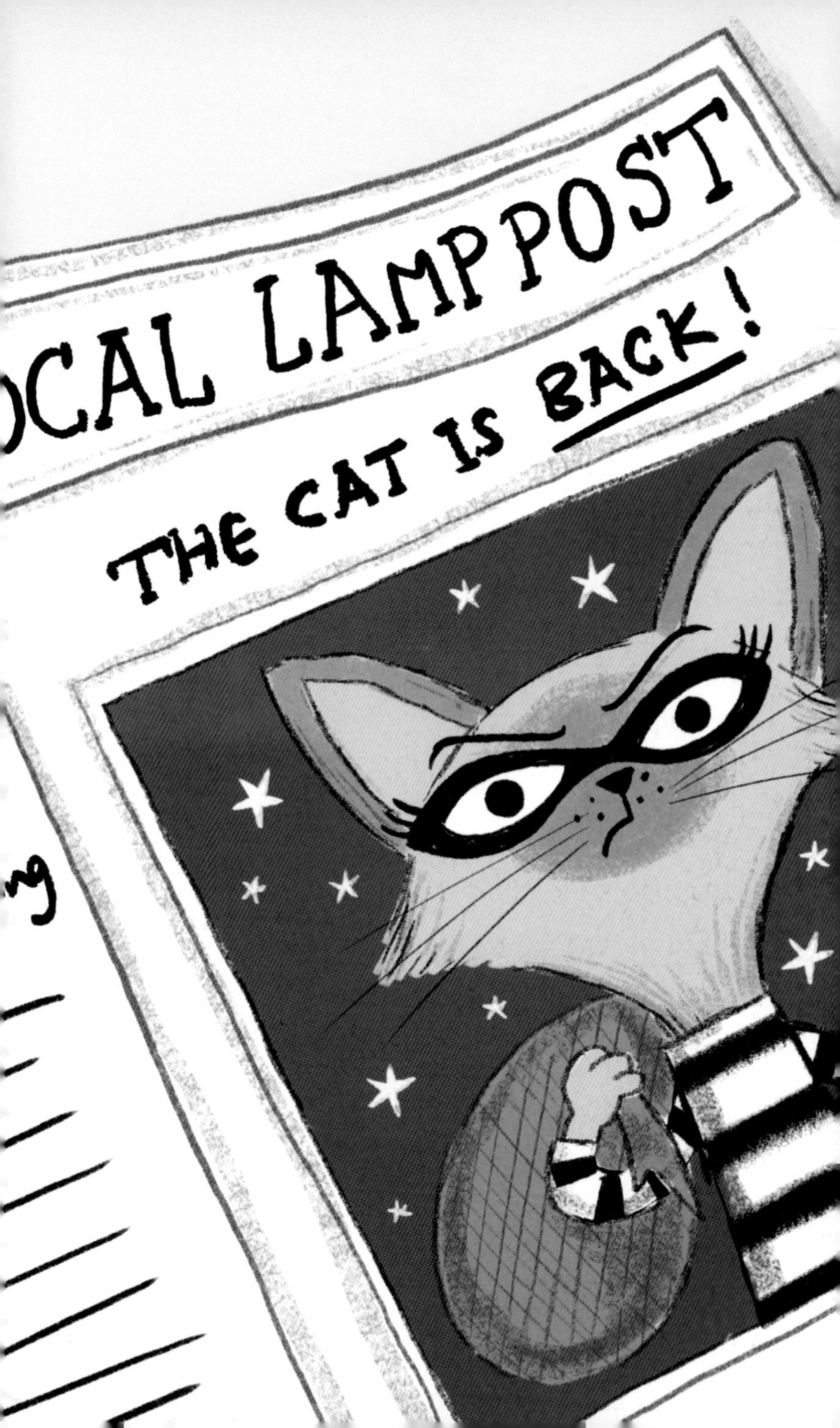
OCAL LAMPPOST
THE CAT IS BACK!

Chapter Four

The boys dived into the Bakemobile and flew down the road after Kitty. Passing shops and houses, they chased her for miles and miles.

Finally she led them to small, quiet airfield where her getaway aeroplane was waiting! Abandoning Fred's car, she dived into the plane and the Bakemobile screeched up beside it.

"Sam – grab the toff-chock!" yelled Shifty.

"Got it!" cried Sam, dashing out of the van with a wedge made from super-hard toffee.

As Kitty started up the aeroplane, Sam stuffed the toff-chock under its front nose-wheel, stopping it from moving along the runway. Kitty was fuming as Shifty rushed over and swiftly pulled open her door.

"Stop meddling!" she shrieked, diving out of the opposite one.

Over her shoulder was a swag bag of treasure belonging to Shifty and Sam's friends. And Kitty also had the hair-braiding gadget she'd used on Rover.

Taking aim, she fired it over her shoulder and a twirl of thick braiding threads shot out. These threads hit Shifty, winding round and round him until he was braided to the spot. Poor Shifty couldn't move.

"Right!" scowled Sam. If Kitty wanted *gadgets* she'd get them...

Racing back to the Bakemobile, Sam opened a flap and pulled out a long green hose.

"Ha! Prepare to be MILKSHAKED!" he sniggered, turning on the hose at once. With a gurgle and a glug, a jet of peach-flavoured milk shot out of the end – Whoosh!!

Kitty tried to outrun it but it swept her off her feet and she landed in an ocean of milky bubbles. "Arrgh!"

119

"Nooooo!" she wailed as a police car screeched up and two big policemen jumped out.

"There you go, officers!" Sam pointed at Kitty. "Miss Peachy-Pie impostor's now a Peach Melba milkshake!" Sam lobbed on a cherry. "And serves her right!"

When Kitty Le Claw had been taken away,
Sam un-braided Shifty by twirling him. Shifty
was so dizzy. Being a hair braid was awful.

"But at least we caught the robber," he said.

"And the police will give back all the stolen things too!" added Sam.

The boys were very pleased with themselves. The Pamper Café would be closed for good so everything could go back to normal. No more bumps and bruises from roller-skate accidents, for the boys could have their good old café back. Just as well too, as they'd completely run out of plasters!

"Well done, Sam," Shifty said.

"You too," smiled Sam. "Now it's time for our reward."

And grabbing the green hose again, he flicked on the switch and...